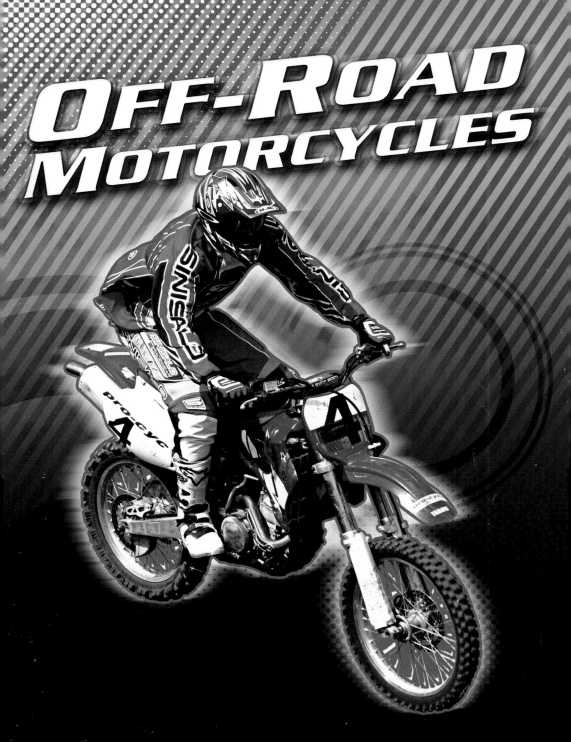

OFF-ROAD MOTORCYCLES

BY THOMAS STREISSGUTH

BELLWETHER MEDIA · MINNEAPOLIS, MN

™

Are you ready to take it to the extreme?
Torque books thrust you into the action-packed
world of sports, vehicles, and adventure.
These books may include dirt, smoke, fire, and
dangerous stunts.
WARNING: Read at your own risk.

Library of Congress Cataloging-in-Publication Data

Streissguth, Thomas, 1958–
    Off-road motorcycles / by Thomas Streissguth.
        p. cm. – (Torque–motorcycles)
    Summary: "Full color photography accompanies engaging information about Off-Road
motorcycles. The combination of high-interest subject matter and light text is intended for
students in grades 3 through 7"–Provided by publisher.
    Includes bibliographical references and index.
    ISBN-13: 978-1-60014-156-0 (hardcover : alk. paper)
    ISBN-10: 1-60014-156-0 (hardcover : alk. paper)
    1. Trail bikes–Juvenile literature. I. Title.

TL441.S768 2008
629.227'5–dc22   2007040746

This edition first published in 2008 by Bellwether Media.

CONTENTS

WHAT IS AN OFF-ROAD MOTORCYCLE?

Off-road motorcycles are tough bikes built for rough riding. Off-road motorcycle riders may have to maneuver sandy ground, fallen branches, boulders, and deep ruts. Muddy slicks can cause a bike to crash in a second.

FAST FACT

ENDURO BIKES ARE ONE OF THE FEW OFF-ROAD MOTORCYCLES THAT MUST BE STREET LEGAL. THEY COME WITH TURN SIGNALS, HEADLIGHTS, AND BRAKE LIGHTS.

Off-road riding has many forms. Riders often want a motorcycle specialized for their chosen style. **Motocross** riders need a bike that can handle bursts of speed and big dirt jumps.

Trials riders need to maneuver around and over obstacles at low speeds. **Enduro** racing takes riders through both off-road **terrain** and city streets.

Some riders just want to take off into the woods or hills on their own. Off-road motorcycles can do it all.

FEATURES

Off-road motorcycles are different from street motorcycles. Most off-road bikes have few **accessories**. Almost all off-road bikes are not street legal. They don't have lights or turn signals.

Off-road bikes don't weigh as much as street bikes. Lightweight bikes are easier to maneuver than heavier bikes.

Off-road bikes differ from street bikes in other key ways. The frames of off-road bikes ride higher off the ground. This helps them get over obstacles. Off-road motorcycle tires have deep **tread** for a better grip on dirt and mud.

FAST FACT

SUPERCROSS EVENTS TAKE PLACE IN INDOOR STADIUMS. THEY ARE LIKE MOTOCROSS RACES ON A SHORTER, TIGHTER COURSE. ORGANIZERS HAUL IN TONS OF DIRT TO SET UP THE COURSE.

The range of movement of a **suspension system** is called its **travel**. Suspension systems on off-road bikes are designed for large bumps and jumps. They have more travel than the suspension systems on street bikes. This means the wheels can move up and down more than the wheels of street bikes to absorb changes in terrain.

Off-road riders maintain control by shifting their weight. A narrow, raised seat and spiked foot pegs allow riders to control their bikes by changing body position.

Safety is important when riding off-road motorycles. Gloves and a helmet are required to protect the rider in case of a crash. Special riding clothes protect the body of a rider if they fall.

OFF-ROAD MOTORCYCLES IN ACTION

Racing is a popular off-road activity. Motocross races take riders around a closed course. The races are intense.

Bikes steer through sharp turns and take steep jumps at high speeds. Riders train hard before racing. They learn to balance and control their bikes while jumping and landing.

A **rally** is an off-road race over a long course. Some rallies cover 1,000 miles (1,609 kilometers) of rugged terrain. One of the most popular rallies is the Buttstomper. It happens every summer in the state of Washington. It lasts 24 hours. Most riders compete in teams of four. One member of the team must complete a full lap around the course every hour. It's a tough test for a rider and his motorcycle.

FAST FACT

THE DAKAR RALLY RUNS THROUGH THE DESERTS AND MOUNTAINS OF AFRICA. IT'S THE TOUGHEST AND MOST DANGEROUS OFF-ROAD MOTORCYCLE EVENT IN THE WORLD. IT IS OFTEN MORE THAN 5,000 MILES (8,000 KILOMETERS) LONG.

GLOSSARY

accessories–extra items to decorate a motorcycle or make it more useful

enduro–a cross-country off-road competition; enduro riders must pass checkpoints at designated times.

motocross–an off-road dirt race through a series of hills and curves

rally–a long-distance road race

suspension system–a series of springs and shock absorbers that connect the frame of a vehicle to its wheels

terrain–the natural surface features of the land

travel–the range of movement of a suspension system; off-road motorcycles have more travel than street motorcycles.

tread–the series of bumps and grooves on a tire that help it grip rough surfaces

trials riders–riders who go through obstacle courses

TO LEARN MORE

AT THE LIBRARY

Budd, E.S. *Off-Road Motorcycles*. Chanhassen, Minn.: Child's World, 2004.

David, Jack. *Dirt Bikes*. Minneapolis, Minn.: Bellwether, 2008.

David, Jack. *Motocross Cycles*. Minneapolis, Minn.: Bellwether, 2008.

David, Jack. *Motocross Racing*. Minneapolis, Minn.: Bellwether, 2008.

ON THE WEB

Learning more about motorcycles is as easy as 1, 2, 3.

1. Go to www.factsurfer.com

2. Enter "motorcycles" into search box.

3. Click the "Surf" button and you will see a list of related web sites.

With factsurfer.com, finding more information is just a click away.

INDEX

The images in this book are reproduced through the courtesy of: Yamaha Motor Corporation, cover, p. 19; American Honda Motor Co., Inc., pp. 6, 10-11, 12, 14 (bottom), 17; KTM Sportmotorcycle AG, pp. 4-5, 7, 8-9, 14 (top), 15, 18, 21-21.